1 2 3

A Family Counting Book

1 2 3

A Family Counting Book

Bobbie Combs

illustrated by Danamarie Hosler

Two Lives Publishing

JE
COM

Published by
Two Lives Publishing
508 North Swarthmore Avenue
Ridley Park, PA 19078

Visit our website: www.twolives.com

Copyright © 2000 by Bobbie Combs
Illustrations copyright © 2000 by Danamarie Hosler

ISBN: 0-9674468-0-5

Library of Congress Cataloging-in-Publication Data
00-190738

1 2 3 4 5 6 7 8 9 10

Printed in Hong Kong

For Sally:
one we're given, and the other one we make . . .
—B.C.

To Ashley,
who continues to teach me the true meaning of family
—D.H.

1

One family going for a ride

2 Two houses with families inside

3

Three books waiting to be read

Four puppies waiting to be fed

5

Five hats sitting on our heads

6 Six cats sleeping on our bed

7

Seven skaters rolling down the street

8

Eight popsicles for a special treat

9

Nine candles on a birthday cake

and **nine** little boxes for the guests to take

10

Ten bubbles floating in the air

11

Eleven toys and a teddy bear

12

Twelve friends swimming in a pool

and twelve parents watching, trying to stay cool

13 Thirteen balloons bouncing on their strings

14 Fourteen butterflies with brightly colored wings

15

Fifteen kites soaring in the sky

and fifteen fluffy clouds watching them go by

16

Sixteen trees for climbing to the top

17

Seventeen frogs teaching us to hop

18

Eighteen feathers scattered on the ground

19 Nineteen seashells waiting to be found

20

Twenty fireflies in the campfire light

and twenty twinkling stars wishing us good night

Bobbie Combs is a children's book consultant and one of the owners of Two Lives Publishing. She lives in Philadelphia, Pennsylvania.

Danamarie Hosler is a graduate of the Maryland Institute College of Art. She lives in Baltimore, Maryland.